PETEY
AND
QUACKERS

David Newell

PAGE PUBLISHING, INC.
Conneaut Lake, PA

First originally published by Page Publishing 2021

ISBN 978-1-6624-5459-2 (hc)
ISBN 978-1-6624-5458-5 (digital)

Printed in the United States of America

To my four best female friends
relatively speaking:
Nadine, Genevra, Harper and Martha

I'm Scott, and chickens are in my blood. I found an old snapshot of my grandfather tending to hundreds of chickens fenced in between two barns right on Main Street during the Great Depression. I hope they were all egg layers because if they were meat birds, I am afraid he might've had lost his shirt. They were the most motley, scrubby-looking birds I had ever seen assembled in one place.

This being my relative history of chickens, it was no surprise when I started my own family that one of the first things I built on our new property was a red barn that could house both my horse and some chickens.

Because happy, adjusted chickens need entertainment, we purchased two ducks. We called the male Hecliff because whenever he was missing, all we had to do was look over the cliff behind the barn, and there he would be. He was a beautiful specimen with green and yellow plumage and was probably one and one half a size bigger than the female duck. His mate, Quackers, did just that all the time, hence her name. They were all one big happy family. The ducks ate what the chickens ate and vice versa.

Time passed, as it does, and the chickens grew and were well adjusted, scurrying around the barn area, sometimes pursued by the earth-grubbing ducks. My horse was enjoying his retirement, usually finding the biggest spot with sunlight in the field to spend the day basking in his glory.

Hecliff's life was short-lived because one night, a fox made his way into the henhouse, and Hecliff, while defending his domain, was carried off to the den. Unfortunately, Quackers was destined to remain a widow for many, many years.

As time went by, ten chickens were replaced each year with new little ones to offset the ones who had flown the coop, so to speak. Quackers welcomed all the many newcomers each year with the gusto of a personal director giving guided tours of the barn.

Quackers did not fare well a couple of times before we moved. She had a very loud run-in with a resident raccoon one night and lost an eye during the fracas. Anyone who has ever had chickens knows how they can react to blood or even an open cut on one another. This being the case, I had to separate Quackers from the girls until her eye socket healed before reintroducing her to the flock.

Bag Balm, an antiseptic that inhibits bacterial growth, worked wonders in speeding up the recovery time. She had a tendency to walk in circles for a while, but she finally readjusted to her missing part.

The first renovations I personally supervised were our henhouse and woodshed. I had kept chickens there as a boy, and it was still in pretty good shape. It was maybe a bit dusty and such but not bad after we cleaned it all out and made some needed interior repairs. I wanted it to be somewhat maintenance-free before I moved the girls down to their new lodgings with Quackers.

It may have been the move or the new digs, but Quackers seemed to never leave the chickens alone. She was forever biting their backsides to move them out of her way.

This didn't last long because the chickens revolted and began to peck her face where her bill met her head. It became so obvious that I had to move her into a separate area just for her protection.

I had constructed a separate area for raising new chicks, and this now was Quackers's new home. It turned into a hospital of sorts for sick chickens that would spend their last days with Quackers before they passed on. Quackers didn't bother them during their convalescence. I think she knew they were defenseless during this confined time. I bet we had at least six or seven chickens that went through this procedure over the next three or four years. I never kill a chicken; I just let them pass on their own. I had one chicken that lived to be thirteen years old.

Spring arrived, as it does, and in the spring, before I start my garden or the flower gardens near the barn, I usually let the chickens out to get some young spring grass, which they love. Quackers was another story. I had to approach her on her blind side before I attempted to catch her and carry her outside. The squawking noises she made as I first touched her would lead the neighbors to believe that I was killing her. Once she was reunited with the chickens, she settled down to a great pasture of green grass. This was her heaven.

At first sign of darkness, the chickens made their way back to their outside enclosed yard followed by Quackers. I would then have to repeat the procedure—capturing her and depositing her back into her designated pen for her own good. This brought on more squawking and loud quacking, but I was used to it.

The summer and part of the fall season passed with no major poultry events, but one October day, I noticed Quackers was walking into every wall in her enclosure. On closer inspection, I saw what I thought was the problem. Her good eye, her only eye, had a rather large growth above it. This growth was restricting her sight and causing her not to see even the four walls of her pen.

Here we go again; now I'm a doctor. I asked one of the high school boys who worked for me to hold Quackers as I attempted, with an X-Acto knife, to remove the excess growth so that she could see again. Bag Balm, the miracle salve for poultry, worked wonders in a few weeks a second time. Quackers was working her circling charm again in her enclosure.

New England winters can be brutal, especially so for all kinds of birds. I diligently began early preparations for winterizing the henhouse and their outside run. I stapled up a plastic barrier on the exterior run to cut back on the sometimes-relentless wind that blew around the back of the barn. I installed electric water heaters and banked up extra shavings inside their pen and Quackers's to ward off any sharp drop in temperatures. Over the years, my efforts have been quite successful, and I can report no loss in habitants because of foul weather, no pun intended.

My sister has some (not sure how many) pigeons in her barn, my old barn, next to her chickens. She feeds them, but for the most part, they tend to their own needs and reproduce quite rapidly on a regular basis. Many times she doesn't even know there are new babies until she cleans their coop. Last spring, unfortunately, she discovered one that had fallen out of its nest some six feet up from the floor. The other pigeons had not welcomed its intrusion with open wings. To put it bluntly, they beat it up. She quickly scooped up the poor creature and took it to her house, deciding to raise it in her spare bathroom.

The new arrival seemed to improve somewhat. The blood smears disappeared and were replaced with new feathers.

My sister thought that after some three weeks of keeping this bird caged inside, it would be time to return it to its original habitat.

However, the welcome mat was not out at the old homestead, and the other pigeons immediately attacked it again to the point where it wasn't going to be able to stay long with its relatives and live.

The very next morning, my sister came to me with a surprise in her coat pocket: the baby pigeon. It was February and cold, and I was at work. What was I going to do with a pigeon? I quickly took the pigeon over to my chicken house and put him in with Quackers. I figured Quackers was legally blind, so at least she wouldn't see the pigeon half the time. He would have a chance of survival.

At the end of the day, I hurriedly checked Quackers's pen and to see if they had gotten along. No pigeon. I went inside the pen to question Quackers. As I think about it, I can't believe I actually thought I could have a conversation with a duck.

"Quackers, where's the pigeon?"

Before Quackers could answer, and that would have been something, she raised her left wing to expose the little pigeon peeking out, warmly nestled under her new friend. We named him Petey.

They got along famously. Petey became Quackers's protector. They slept together, they ate together, and I even witnessed them walking in circles together.

When I had to place a sick chicken in with them, I could almost hear Petey cooing to the intruder, 'Stay in your comer. We will stay in ours. And don't come over here. You're sick, and we don't want to catch whatever it is that you have."

Petey always stayed on the good-eye side of Quackers so that she would know where he was at all times. It worked.

Petey liked to dance or put on a little show now and then. I think it was more of a mating call than a dance, but whatever. My wife and I decided that maybe Petey was lonely, so we installed a mirror about a foot off the floor so he could see his image while he danced. Well, Arthur Murray, step aside because Petey outdanced them all with high flips, wings spread out, and beautiful one-foot landings. Quackers loved it all, and I could see her webbed feet move from time to time as if they were tapping.

I eventually cut a pigeonhole into the outside wire pen and introduced Petey to the rest of the chickens. There have been a couple of incidents between Petey and a few chickens, but on the whole, he has held his own quite well. Petey knows he can fly up to his separate entrance away from his new friends when needed, which at first was often. He never stayed away too long, especially when dusk was approaching, but more importantly, he wanted to be with Quackers when it was time for bed. They both shared the same back corner under the feeding station night after night. Petey usually rested his head on Quackers for the entire night like he was there to protect her.

Quackers was about fourteen at this juncture in her life, and the years were starting to show in her movements and, at times, her attitude. Petey respected her moods and knew when to avoid her altogether.

She still quacked when I picked her up and took her outside, and she repeated the process when I returned her to her safe haven with Petey. But she didn't fight or squirm as hard as usual. She was physically slowing down.

We all made it through the summer, on to the first signs of winter, and to our first snowfall, which turned out to be a dusting.

I had noticed that Quackers really wasn't leaving her corner much and that Petey was right there most of the time. I had seen Petey pick up more coarse cracked corn at night than he could eat, so I watched him bring it to Quackers in the corner and place it in front of her. I don't know how long this went on, but I suspect it had been going on for some time. Petey was now the caregiver, and Quackers was the patient.

I suspected that Quackers's days were numbered because I had to move her a couple times just to clean her corner and replace her shavings with new bedding. Petey didn't help at all. In fact, he hindered the work by trying to bite my gloves during the clean-out time. As soon as I had finished the cleaning and directed Quackers back to her corner, Petey was right there, spread-eagled over the duck. "I can take it from here," I thought I heard him say.

Two days later, Quackers left this world for another place. To be honest, she may have passed earlier, but I was so used to Petey lying over her all day that it never crossed my mind that she had died. There was no movement below Petey, and she always responded to him.

Removing Quackers from the pen was going to be another event I wasn't looking forward to. Petey was not in the mood to give up anything, and that included Quackers.

I finally convinced my wife that she would have to catch Petey, hold him, and turn him away from the corner so that I could remove Quackers's body from the pen. This was what we did.

Now the fun began. Petey was a disaster. He would not stop talking, he would not stop pacing, and he made short, dangerous flights back and forth in the pen, always ending up at their corner. He hated his mirror. What's the use? There was no one left to entertain. Evening was approaching, and we were slightly worried about how well Petey would do on his first night alone.

I credit my wife for coming up with a brilliant solution: "Get a fake stuffed duck and put it in their corner." It worked. Petey took to the stuffed duck like a charm. It didn't take too long for Petey to rest his head on it as he had done with Quackers and settle down for the night.

I handcrafted a small wooden box for Quackers with a slight modification. Under her right side, I installed a small elevation that lifted her body to one side; it was as if she was looking to the left for something she had lost. When (and I hope not soon) Petey follows, his box will be of the opposite construction so that they will look at each other through eternity.

About the Author

David Newell Sr. was born into a large family and raised in Woodbury, Connecticut. As a boy, he always had chickens. He had an egg route and a paper route. He is a former English teacher and also owned a local family hardware and feed store until his retirement. His younger sister introduced him to pigeons. Petey, a pigeon, is one of the leading characters in this story.

About the Illustrator

Bonny Hartigan grew up in Burlington, Connecticut, where she roamed the forests, enjoying nature. She was inspired while watching her mom paint local landscapes and helping her dad in his woodworking business.

She taught elementary art for thirty years, which furthered her love for drawing animals, especially horses. She continues to exhibit in local art galleries.

CPSIA information can be obtained
at www.ICGtesting.com
Printed in the USA
LVHW050708231221
706779LV00002B/5